DATE DUE

NOV 9 '04			
JAN 17 '05			
NOV 23 '09			
NOV 13 '13			

I'm Good At

I'm Good at Helping

Eileen M. Day

Heinemann Library
Chicago, Illinois

Customer Service 888-454-2279
Visit our website at www.heinemannlibrary.com

Designed by Sue Emerson, Heinemann Library; Page layout by Que-Net Media
Printed and bound in the United States by Lake Book Manufacturing, Inc.
Photo research by Alan Gottlieb and Amor Montes de Oca

07 06 05 04 03
10 9 8 7 6 5 4 3 2 1

Library of Congress Cataloging-in-Publication Data
Day, Eileen.
  I'm good at helping / Eileen Day.
       p. cm. — (I'm good at)
Includes index.
Summary: Explains what it means and how it feels to be helpful, and shows how to help at home and in other locations.
  ISBN 1-4034-0897-1 (HC), 1-4034-3445-X (Pbk.)
  1. Helping behavior—Juvenile literature. [1. Helpfulness.] I. Title: I am good at helping. II. Title. II. Series.
  BF637.H4 D29 2003
  177'.7—dc21

                              2002014731

Acknowledgments
The author and publishers are grateful to the following for permission to reproduce copyrighted material:
p. 4 Scott Barrow/International Stock; pp. 5, 7 Norbert Schafer/Corbis; pp. 6, 18 PhotoDisc; p. 8 Lawrence Migdale/Stock Boston; p. 9 Taxi/Getty Images; p. 10 EyeWire/Getty Images; p. 11 Ariel Skelley/Corbis; p. 12 George Shelley/Corbis; p. 13 David Young-Wolff/Photo Edit; p. 14 Craig Hammell/Corbis; p. 15 Pictor, International; p. 16 Mrs. Kevin Scheibel Photography; p. 17 Bob Daemmrich Photo, Inc.; p. 19 Richard Hutchings/PhotoEdit; p. 20 Digital Vision/Getty Images; p. 21 (row 1, L-R) Norbert Schafer/Corbis, Ariel Skelley/Corbis; p. 21 (row 2, L-R) Craig Hammell/Corbis, David Young-Wolff/Photo Edit; pp. 22, 24 Robert Lifson/Heinemann Library; p. 23 (T-B) George Shelley/Corbis, PhotoDisc, Corbis, Digital Vision/Getty Images; back cover (L-R) George Shelley/Corbis, Pictor, International

Cover photograph by Tom & Dee Ann McCarthy/Corbis

Special thanks to our advisory panel for their help in the preparation of this book:

Alice Bethke,
Library Consultant
Palo Alto, CA

Kathleen Gilbert,
Second Grade Teacher
Round Rock, TX

Sandra Gilbert,
Library Media Specialist
Fiest Elementary School
Houston, TX

Jan Gobeille,
Kindergarten Teacher
Garfield Elementary
Oakland, CA

Angela Leeper,
Educational Consultant
North Carolina Department
of Public Instruction
Wake Forest, NC

Some words are shown in bold, **like this.**
You can find them in the picture glossary on page 23.

Contents

What Is Helping?

Helping is doing something for someone else.

There are helpers in my neighborhood.

4

I can help at home.

I can help in my neighborhood, too.

How Do I Help at Home?

I can help Mom make dinner.

We can make a **pizza**.

Later, I can help clean the kitchen.

I can help with the dishes.

How Do I Help at the Grocery Store?

We go to the grocery store to buy food.

I put the fruit in the bag.

We can help Mom at the grocery store.

We put food in the cart.

How Do I Help My Sister?

At the beach, I can help my sister build a **sand castle.**

I put **sand** in a bucket.

At home, I can help my sister give our dog a bath.

She sprays water on our dog.

How Do I Help Outside?

I can help plant a **garden**.

We will grow flowers and vegetables.

First, I dig a hole.

Then, I put in a **seed**.

How Do I Help My Neighborhood?

I can help keep the park clean.

I can put trash in the can.

I can sweep the sidewalk.

I can rake the fall leaves.

How Do I Help My Neighbor?

My neighbor lives in the house next door.

I can bring her newspaper to her.

I can take her dog for a walk.

I like to help my neighbor.

How Do I Help at School?

I can help my teacher.

I can tell her the date.

I can help our class pet.

I give it food to eat.

How Do I Feel When I Help?

Helping makes me feel happy.

It makes other people happy, too.

I can help every day.

When I help it makes me smile!

Quiz

How can you help?

Look for the answer on page 24.

Picture Glossary

garden
page 12

sand castle
page 10

pizza
page 6

seed
page 13

sand
page 10

Note to Parents and Teachers

Reading for information is an important part of a child's literacy development. Learning begins with a question about something. Help children think of themselves as investigators and researchers by encouraging their questions about the world around them. Each chapter in this book begins with a question. Read the question together. Look at the pictures. Talk about what you think the answer might be. Then read the text to find out if your predictions were correct. Think of other questions you could ask about the topic, and discuss where you might find the answers. Assist children in using the picture glossary and the index to practice new vocabulary and research skills.

Index

Answer to quiz on page 22
You can put trash in the trash can.